Before reading

Look at the book cover
Ask, "What do you thin[k]

Turn to the **Key Words**
the child. Draw their attention to the ~~~~
the tall letters and those that have a tail.

During reading

Offer plenty of support and praise as the child reads the story. Listen carefully and respond to events in the text.

When a **Key Word** is used for the first time, it is also shown at the bottom of the page. If the child hesitates over a word, point to the **New Key Words** box and practise reading it together. If the word is phonically decodable, you can sound out the letters and blend the sounds to read the word ("d-o-g, dog"). Praise the child for their effort, then return to the story.

Pause every few pages and ask questions to check the child's understanding of what they have read. If they begin to lose concentration, stop reading and save the page for later.

Celebrate the child's achievement and come back to the story the next day.

After reading

After reading this book, ask, "Did you enjoy the story? What did you like about it?" Encourage the child to share their opinions.

Use the comprehension questions on page 54 to check the child's understanding and recall of the text.

Ladybird

Series Consultant: Professor David Waugh
With thanks to Kulwinder Maude

LADYBIRD BOOKS

UK | USA | Canada | Ireland | Australia
India | New Zealand | South Africa

Ladybird Books is part of the Penguin Random House group of companies whose addresses can be found at global.penguinrandomhouse.com.
www.penguin.co.uk   www.puffin.co.uk   www.ladybird.co.uk

 Penguin Random House UK

Original edition of Key Words with Peter and Jane first published by Ladybird Books Ltd 1964
Series updated 2023
This book first published 2023
004

Text copyright © Ladybird Books Ltd, 1964, 2023
Illustrations by Nuno Alexandre Vieira
Based on characters and design by Gustavo Mazali
Illustrations copyright © Ladybird Books Ltd, 2023

No part of this book may be used or reproduced in any manner for the purpose of training artificial intelligence technologies or systems. In accordance with Article 4(3) of the DSM Directive 2019/790, Penguin Random House expressly reserves

Printed in China

The authorized representative in the EEA is Penguin Random House Ireland, Morrison Chambers, 32 Nassau Street, Dublin D02 YH68

A CIP catalogue record for this book is available from the British Library

ISBN: 978-0-241-51076-6

All correspondence to:
Ladybird Books
Penguin Random House Children's
One Embassy Gardens, 8 Viaduct Gardens, London SW11 7BW

with Peter and Jane

Jump in!

Based on the original
Key Words with Peter and Jane
reading scheme and research by William Murray

Original edition written by William Murray
This edition written by Zoë Clarke
Illustrated by Nuno Alexandre Vieira
Based on characters and design by Gustavo Mazali

Key Words

are   can   come

fish   fun   have

it   jump   look

on   say   she

they   want

water   you

Here are Jane and Peter.

New Key Words

are

Look! They are in the water.

New Key Words

look they water

The water is fun.

They have a ball in the water.

New Key Words

fun   have

They have fun.

You can have fun.

It is fun in the water.

New Key Words

you   can   it

Jane looks in the water.

"Can you come and look, Peter?" she says.

New Key Words

come   she   say

Peter looks in
the water.

"It is a fun fish,"
Peter says.

New Key Words

fish

Peter wants the fish.

"The fish looks fun. I want it," Peter says.

New Key Words

want

Jane has a
fish net.

"Come and look.
I have a fish net,"
she says.

New Key Words

"Come on. You can have it, Peter," Jane says.

New Key Words

on

Peter dips the fish
net in the water.

New Key Words

"You have it! You have the fish!" Jane says.

New Key Words

"Look, it jumps!
It is a fun fish,"
Peter says.

New Key Words

jump

Jane jumps.

"I can jump like a fish!" she says.

New Key Words

"Come on! You can have fun," says Jane.

New Key Words

"I can jump in the water!" Peter says.

Peter and Jane are like fish!

New Key Words

They have a
fun game.

New Key Words

"Come on! Come and jump on here!" Jane says.

New Key Words

Jane can jump.

She can jump in
the water.

New Key Words

"You can jump, Peter! Come and jump in the water!" Jane says.

New Key Words

It looks fun.

Peter can jump
on it.

New Key Words

Peter can jump.

"Look! I can jump in the water!" says Peter.

New Key Words

"You are fun,"
says Jane.

"You are fun!"
says Peter.

New Key Words

They like the water.

It is fun!

New Key Words

Questions

Answer these questions about the story.

1 What can Jane see in the water?

2 How does Peter get it out of the water?

3 What do Peter and Jane jump on?